An Animal Family

CHICKENS AND CHICKS

By Emilia Hendrix

Gareth Stevens
PUBLISHING

Please visit our website, www.garethstevens.com. For a free color catalog of all our high-quality books, call toll free 1-800-542-2595 or fax 1-877-542-2596.

Cataloging-in-Publication Data

Hendrix, Emilia.
Chickens and chicks / by Emilia Hendrix.
p. cm. — (An animal family)
Includes index.
ISBN 978-1-4824-3771-3 (pbk.)
ISBN 978-1-4824-3772-0 (6-pack)
ISBN 978-1-4824-3773-7 (library binding)
1. Chickens — Juvenile literature. I. Title.
SF487.5 H46 2016
636.5—d23

First Edition

Published in 2016 by
Gareth Stevens Publishing
111 East 14th Street, Suite 349
New York, NY 10003

Editor: Ryan Nagelhout
Designer: Andrea Davison-Bartolotta

Photo credits: Cover, p. 1 Pozukhov Yuriy/Shutterstock.com; pp. 5, 15, 24 (eggs) Volodymyr Baleha/Shutterstock.com; p. 7 christiangda/iStock/Thinkstock; pp. 9, 24 (hen) leisuretime70/iStock/Thinkstock; p. 11 AnaishaClicks/iStock/Thinkstock; p. 13 © iStockphoto.com/northlightimages; p. 17 therry/iStock/Thinkstock; p. 19 © iStockphoto.com/Naruden; pp. 21, 24 (shell) Anneka/Shutterstock.com; p. 23 PCHT/Shutterstock.com.

Printed in the United States of America

CPSIA compliance information: Batch #CW16GS: For further information contact Gareth Stevens, New York, New York at 1-800-542-2595.

Contents

Farm Family 4
Cute Chicks 10
Hens and Eggs 12
Heating Up. 16
Words to Know 24
Index. 24

Many chickens live on farms. They have a family there.

Chickens are birds.
They have wings.

Mother chickens are called hens.

Their babies are called chicks.

Hens lay eggs.
They have about
one egg per day!

Not all eggs are white!
They are many colors.

Eggs need
to stay warm.

Hens sit on their eggs. This keeps them warm.

Chicks have to come out of their shells.

Chicks are very fuzzy!

Words to Know

eggs

hen

shell

Index

chicks 10, 20, 22

eggs 12, 14, 16, 18

hens 8, 12, 18

shells 20